This Orq.

He live in cave.

He carry club.

He cave boy.

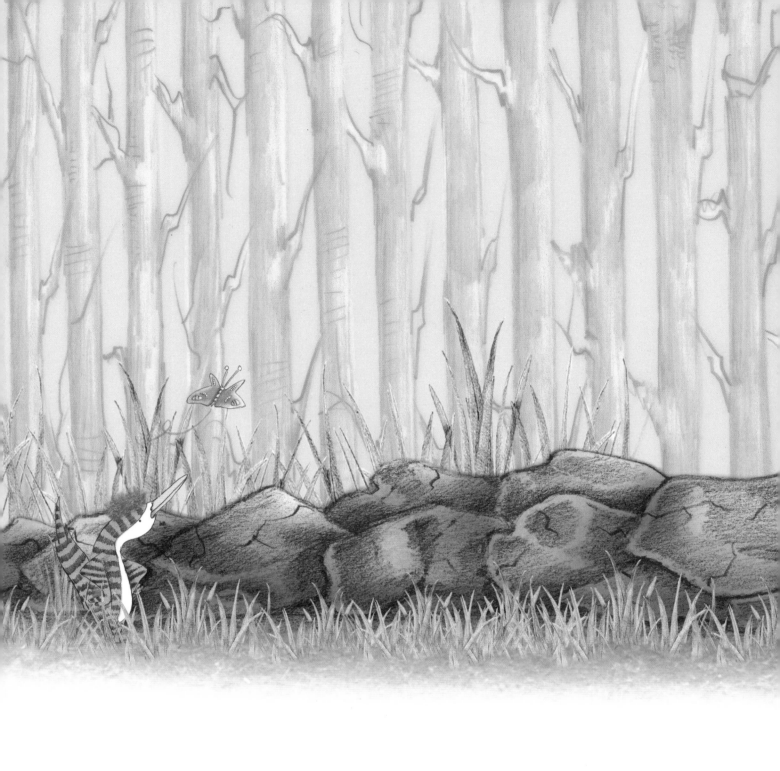

This Woma.

Woma woolly mammoth.

Orq **love** Woma.

Every day Woma grow **bigger** . . .

and **bigger** ...

. . . and
bigger!

Orq
love
Woma.

But Orq's mother
not so sure.
Woma shed.

Woma smell.

Woma not house-trained.

Mother say,
"Get that woolly
mammoth out of
this cave!"

Poor Woma.

Orq **love** Woma.

Orq get **big** idea.
Teach Woma tricks.
Mother think Woma clever.
Mother think Woma cute.
Mother *love* Woma.

"Speak, Woma! Speak!"

"Fetch, Woma! Fetch!"

"Roll over, Woma! Roll o—"

Poor Woma!

Orq **love** Woma.

One day, Orq playing.
He mighty hunter!
Hunt bison!
Hunt cave bear!

Hunt . . .

. . . sabretooth!

Poor Orq!

Sabretooth **love** Orq. But . . .

. . . Woma **love** Orq more!
Sabretooth think again.

Orq safe now.

Woma **big** hero.

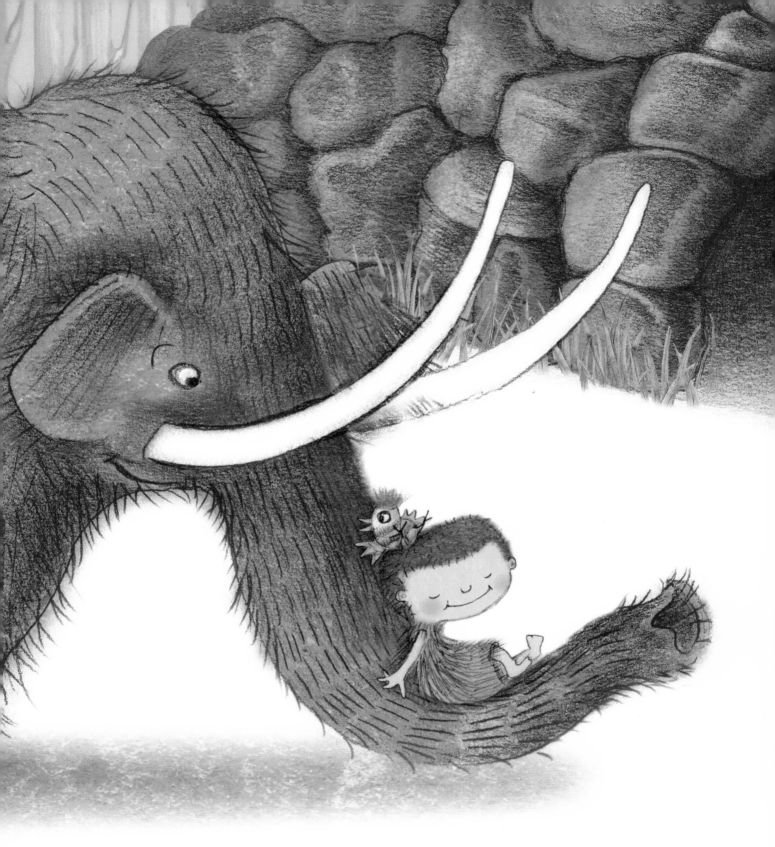

Mother **love** Woma.
Woma back in cave.

Sort of.